Snail,
Where Are
You?

Snail, Where Are You?

Tomi Ungerer

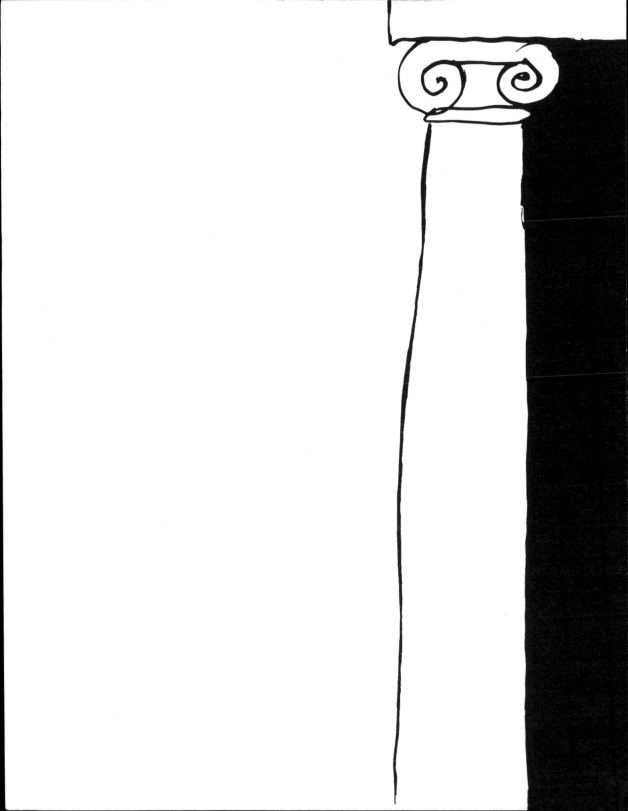

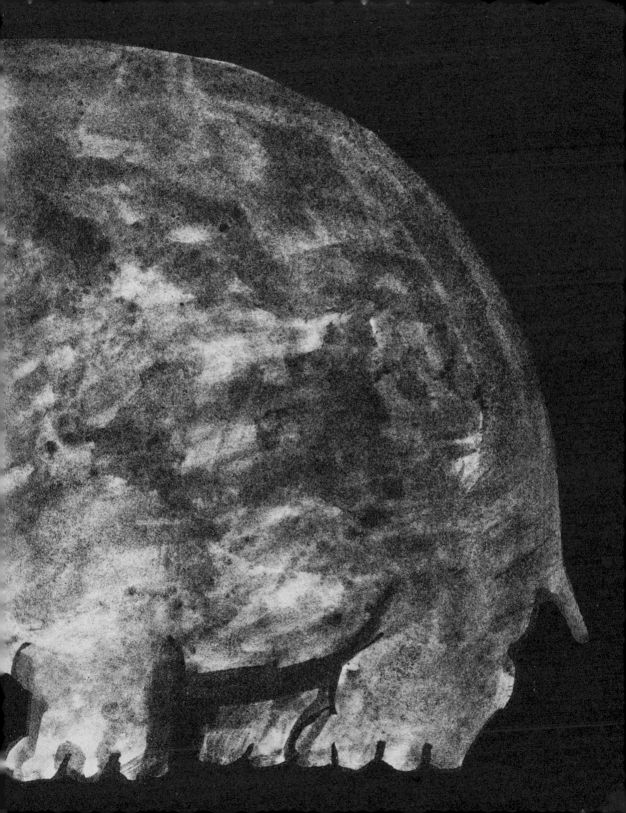

Snail

where are you?

Where has snail gone? Look closely – can you see his shell?

Enjoy finding the hiding snail in every page of this witty and wacky game of hide-and-seek.

Tomi Ungerer (b. 1931) is one of the world's most famous and best-loved children's authors. A recipient of the Hans Christian Andersen Award for illustration, he divides his time between Ireland and Strasbourg, France.

Other titles by Tomi Ungerer published by Phaidon:

- Adelaide: The Flying Kangaroo
- The Beast of Monsieur Racine
- Christmas Eve at the Mellops'
- Fog Island
- The Mellops Go Diving for Treasure
- The Mellops Strike Oil
- Moon Man
- No Kiss for Mother
- One, Two, Where's My Shoe?
- Otto: The Autobiography of a Teddy Bear
- The Three Robbers

Phaidon Press Limited
Regent's Wharf
All Saints Street
London, N1 9PA

Phaidon Press Inc.
65 Bleecker Street
New York, NY 10012

phaidon.com

This edition © 2015 Phaidon Press Limited
First published in German as Schnecke, wo bist du? © 1973 Diogenes Verlag AG Zürich

ISBN 978 0 7148 6799 1
007-0215

Printed in China